A Gift For:

From:

"For Allie, the best little bedtime-snuggling, bunny chasing, belly-rub loving doggy our family could've hoped for. Love you, Allie girl."

—Kara

Editorial Director: Delia Berrigan
Art Director: Chris Opheim
Designer: Dan Horton

ISBN: 978-1-63059-908-9
1VTD1492

Made in China

0916

A Tail From the HEART

A Story About Puppy Love

By Kara Goodier
Illustrated by Elizabeth Savanella

See those people? They're the best—
my loving family.
That means I belong to them
and they belong to me.

Maya is my favorite,
although telling her is tough.
I want to say, "I love you,"
but as a dog, it's *ruff*.

When I try to tell her
as we snuggle in her bed . . .

she doesn't want to listen!
She just covers up her head.

When I bring my favorite toy
for both of us to share . . .

Maya tugs it from my mouth,
and throws it in the air!

This isn't going how I planned,
but I know what I'll do—
I'll give her LOTS of kisses!
That should do it!

Well, if she doesn't hear me,
and she doesn't want to play,
and she wipes off all my kisses . . .
then I'll find *another* way.

Look what I found! Her favorite toy!
But why is it outdoors?
Who knew that this would be the thing
that I was looking for?!

I bark out, "Hey Maya!
You should come see what I found!"

This time she *listens!* So I scoop
the toy up off the ground.

I carry the toy gently,
and she gives it a soft tug.

But instead of tossing it away,
she gives me a big hug!

I give her joyful kisses . . .

and this time she laughs and giggles!
And when she gives me a kiss, too,
my tail and I both wiggle.

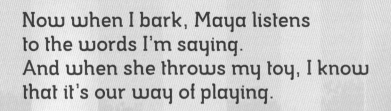

Now when I bark, Maya listens
to the words I'm saying.
And when she throws my toy, I know
that it's our way of playing.

I guess she always understood
what I was trying to do—
all along, in our own ways,
we've both been saying, "I love you."

If you have enjoyed this book
or it has touched your life in some way,
we would love to hear from you.

Please send your comments to:
Hallmark Book Feedback
P.O. Box 419034
Mail Drop 100
Kansas City, MO 64141

Or e-mail us at:
booknotes@hallmark.com